First published in the United States in 1989 by
Ideals Publishing Corporation, Nashville, Tennessee.

First published in Great Britain in 1989 by
Walker Books Ltd.

© 1989 by Jez Alborough

Printed and bound by L.E.G.O., Vicenza, Italy

ISBN 0-8249-8358-0

CUPBOARD

BEAR

Written and illustrated by

JEZ ALBOROUGH

IDEALS CHILDREN'S BOOKS
Nashville, Tennessee

Bear should fix that broken pane —

it dribbles drops of snow and rain.

But jobs like that are always kept
till after lazy Bear has slept.

He dreams of slipping out the back

to fetch himself an icy snack.

But what a shock when he gets there,

the ice cream's gone—

the cupboard's bare!

As he turns and starts to shout,

a pile of snow falls on his snout.

At least, that is, he thinks it's snow.
It feels too thick and sticky, though,

and tastes of sugar. Can it mean...

it's snowing blobs of white ice cream?

It's twice as nice as snow or ice;

it's Bear's idea of paradise.

Before he tries to eat it all,

he makes himself a little ball,

then rolls it into something grand...

the biggest scoop

all the land!

But suddenly it starts to slip,

and Bear begins to lose his grip.

Now it's time without delay…

to make a speedy getaway.

He sees a rock—too late to dodge—

rolls over once and...

WATCH OUT!

SPLODGE!

"Ice cream!" he screams.
"Ice cream, ice cream!

Thank heavens, it was all a dream."

Now he does not hesitate;
the household chores will have to wait.

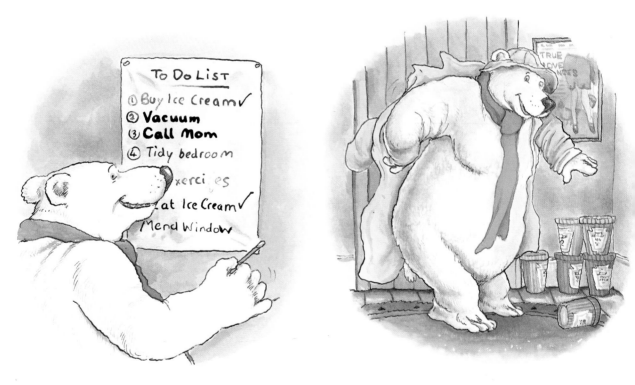

Broken windows should be fixed...

but work and pleasure
can't be mixed.